How to be a hero

This book is not like others you have read. This is a choose-your-own-destiny book where YOU are the hero of the adventure.

Each section of this book is numbered. At the end of most sections, you will have to make a choice. Each choice will take you to a different section of the book.

If you choose correctly, you will succeed. But be careful. If you make a bad choice, you may have to start the adventure again. If this happens, make sure you learn from your mistake!

Go to the next page to start your adventure. And remember, don't be a zero, be a hero!

You are Sapphire, a magical unicorn who lives in Rainbow Land with two other unicorns, Carmine and Emerald.

Each of you has a coloured horn, which you can use to cast spells. Your horn is blue, Carmine's is red and Emerald's is green. When you all meet together, the magical light that shines from your horns produces all the colours of the rainbow to keep Rainbow Land happy, prosperous and free from evil.

Your country lies next to the Land of Shadows, a kingdom ruled by Empress Yin Yang. Her realm has no colour: everything is black and white. She hates everything that is colourful and despises Rainbow Land. Luckily, a magical wall of colour keeps the two kingdoms apart, stopping the empress from destroying your land. But you know that you must always be on your guard to defend Rainbow Land from the empress's wicked plans.

Go to 1.

It is the time of year when you and the other unicorns meet together to renew the power of the magical rainbow that spreads colour throughout Rainbow Land.

You canter into the magic meadow, where you are meeting with Emerald and Carmine, but when you arrive only Emerald is there.

"Where is Carmine?" you ask.

Emerald shakes her head. "I thought she was with you."

"I haven't seen her for several days," you reply. "This isn't like her to disappear. We should search for her."

"Perhaps Lady Harmony will know where she is," suggests Emerald.

Lady Harmony is the queen of the elves and has a magic crystal. She can use it to see what is happening across Rainbow Land.

To search for Carmine, go to 14.

To ask Lady Harmony for help, go to 37.

2

You allow a goblin to place a chain around your neck. He ties you to a marble pillar next to the one where Carmine is tied.

A giant with an axe moves towards you and raises it above your head.

If you want to return to the Grotto of Light, go to 26.

If you want to wait, go to 29.

3

You decide to rest. You sink to the ground and close your eyes to sleep and recover some energy.

After some time, you suddenly wake with a start and see a group of dwarves standing over you. You try to leap up, but you can't — you are trapped in a shadownet. The dwarves tighten the net and you feel your magical powers being drained from you...

Go to 26.

4

"You will need this to help you in your quest to rescue Carmine," says Lady Harmony. She places a golden crown on your head.

"If you are in danger and cannot escape, then call upon the power of the Golden Heart Crown. It will bring you back to this time and place. It will also help you when you find Carmine. Touch your horn to hers and Emerald will be summoned to your side.

Now you must hurry and rescue Carmine before the rainbow colours leave our land forever."

You say goodbye to Emerald and Lady Harmony and head to the border. Ahead of you is the magical wall of colour that divides your kingdom from the Land of Shadows. You have never been through it before...

To try to break through the wall by force, go to 46.

To use magic to break through, go to 10.

5

You move further into the mountains and eventually reach a vast waterfall that tumbles down from towering cliffs. There is no way around or over the wall of water. It seems as though you have reached a dead end!

If you talked to the goblins at the border, go to 30.

If you didn't, go to 26.

6

You head towards the Gloomy Mountains, following the course of the Black River.

After travelling for some hours, you begin to make your way into the mountains. Ravens and crows watch you progress up a rocky and treacherous path, but they do not attack.

Eventually you find yourself at a wooden bridge spanning a deep ravine. On the bridge stands a fearsome-looking black knight mounted on a huge rhinoceros.

To use magic on the knight, go to 32.
To attack the knight, go to 45.

"Is there more to see?" you ask.

"We must ask the crystal," replies Lady Harmony. "Crystal, please reveal who is behind this." There is another explosion of colour and then the black-and-white image of a woman appears. It is the Empress Yin Yang!

"So you have discovered that my followers have taken your red unicorn," Yin Yang says, grinning. "But this is only the beginning! I know that if your unicorns cannot renew the rainbow, then all the colour in your land will fade to black and white. Then I will become ruler!"

To try to talk to the empress, go to 28.
To make a plan to rescue Carmine, go to 42.

8

You call on your magic powers, but nothing happens.

You stand confused as the empress laughs. "Bring me a mirror," she orders.

A goblin obeys and the empress holds it out. You see that your horn is turning from blue to black!

"Your powers are weakening! Your rainbow is fading! Soon it will be gone and and I will rule your land!" the empress cries. "Chain it up, then chop off both their horns!"

To return to the Grotto of Light, go to 26.

To let them chain you, go to 2.

9

You call on the power of the unicorn and your horn glows bright sapphire. A stream of blue light blasts out and hits the incoming birds with such a force that they crash to the ground, dazed.

You see the eagle and trot up to it. It lies defeated before you. "Where will I find the Dark Palace?" you demand.

"In the Gloomy Mountains," it replies.

You realise that you were heading the wrong way! This cloud of birds has had a silver lining!

Go to 6.

"By the power of the unicorn, please open the way," you command.

Your horn glows blue and a shower of sapphire stars appear. They swirl around, attaching themselves to the wall and open a gap in it.

As you pass through the opening, the hole closes behind you, stopping any beings from the Land of Shadows getting into Rainbow Land.

You gallop into the world of black and white when suddenly a troop of mean-looking goblins steps out of the trees. They are armed and dangerous!

To fight the goblins, go to 34.
To use your magic powers, go to 48.

"Bow your heads," you tell Carmine and Emerald. They do and your three horns touch.

"Bring colour to this land," you say.

There is a flash of light and a blast of air sucks all of the darkness from the room, forming a great cloud. There is a crack of thunder and a deluge of rain pours down. Then it suddenly stops and a mighty rainbow fills the hall with a shower of stars.

You look around to see that every creature has become a colour of the rainbow!

The empress screams. "I hate colours! You've ruined my kingdom!"

Her followers all laugh — they are happy to be released from the Land of Shadows.

Go to 50.

12

You head into the forest, making your way down the narrow track.

As you trot through the trees you instinctively feel that there is danger ahead.

You come to a halt and peer into the darkness. You can just make out the shape of a fallen tree trunk blocking the way ahead. You wonder if this is a trap.

To jump over the trunk, go to 35.
To inspect the trunk, go to 23.

13

You slice through the silken threads with you horn, just as the spider leaps towards you. You rear up and flail at the creature with your hooves, knocking it across the tunnel. It slams into a wall and drops unconscious to the floor.

You hurry away before the spider can wake up. Soon you find yourself at the opening that leads to the secret valley.

In the middle of the valley stands the Dark Palace.

However, between you and the palace is the empress's army. There are thousands of different types of creatures camped in the valley. You wonder how you will get past this army.

You see a pool of water and bend down to take a drink, but at that moment you hear a deep growl. You see a sloth of angry black bears, moving towards you! They have huge razor-sharp claws.

If you decide to gallop away from the bears, go to 36.

If you wish to use your magic to fight the bears, go to 47.

If you decide to surrender to your enemies, go to 27.

14

"Emerald, let us search for Carmine ourselves," you say. "I will head north and west, you head south and east."

You set off, but after hours of searching, you return to the meadow. Emerald has also had no luck finding Carmine.

"This is no good. We must ask Lady Harmony for help," you decide.

Go to 37.

15

You charge at your foe. The knight grabs you in his huge hand and lifts you into the air and over the side of the bridge. You plummet helplessly towards the dark water far below.

Go to 26.

16

"Can you tell me where the red unicorn has been taken?" you ask.

The goblins try not to reply, but your magic makes them answer your question.

"To the Dark Palace of the empress," one of them growls.

"And how do I get there, please?" you continue.

The goblins grit their teeth, trying not to reveal the location of the palace, but they are helpless against your magical powers. "Follow the Black River into the Gloomy Mountains. You will come to a great waterfall. Go through the water and you will find a secret passageway leading to a hidden valley. The Dark Palace is there..."

"Thanks for your co-operation," you laugh. The goblins howl in fury as you gallop away.

Go to 31.

17

"Follow me," you tell Carmine and Emerald.

You race towards the great marble doors, but before you reach them they are slammed shut. You will have to use magic to escape!

Go to 11.

18

Lady Harmony turns to you. "You were brave enough to talk to the empress, and so I choose you." Emerald looks disappointed.

"We need you here," you tell her. "I will bring Carmine back."

Go to 4.

19

You are led to the Dark Palace by the bears. You are taken to the great hall, which is full of dozens of different creatures and beings: goblins, knights, ravens and giants all stare at you as you enter.

Sitting on a great marble throne is the

Empress Yin Yang and tethered to a white marble pillar is Carmine.

"Bring the blue unicorn to me," demands the empress.

To attack the empress, go to 8.
To try to free Carmine, go to 40.

20

You race away, but the birds are too quick for you. They smash into you with such force that you crash to the ground. The birds engulf you, surrounding you in a cloud of black and white feathers...

Go to 26.

21

"By the power of the unicorn, close the wall," you cry. Your horn turns bright blue and a shower of stars stream from it to close the hole, stopping the goblins from entering Rainbow Land.

They turn angrily towards you.

To fight the goblins, go to 34.
To use your magic powers, go to 48.

22

Again you call on your magic powers, but this time you aim your beam of blue light at the wooden bridge beneath the mounted black knight. As the bridge begins to break up, you charge at your enemy and leap over him.

You land on the other side, just as the bridge collapses, sending your foe crashing into the river below.

Go to 5.

23

"Light the way!" you command. Your horn turns blue and illuminates the track.

You walk carefully up to the tree trunk and peer over. You see the outline of a net lying in the middle of the track covered with leaves and twigs. It was a trap!

You walk around the trunk, avoiding the net and continue through the forest.

Sometime later you reach the edge of the forest. Ahead of you is a vast plain. There is a range of gloomy-looking mountains to the west. A black river flows from them towards the east.

If you wish to follow the river to the mountains, go to 6.

If you wish to travel away from the mountains, go to 41.

24

"We must rescue Carmine!" you cry.

"I know you are anxious to save your friend," says Lady Harmony, "but we need to know more."

You realise that she is right.

Go to 7.

25

You race over to Carmine and slice through her chains with your horn. "Lower your head," you tell her.

She bends down and you place your horn against hers. "By the power of the Golden Heart Crown, bring our sister to us!" you cry.

There is an explosion of golden light and colour, which finally dies down to reveal Emerald standing before you!

To attack the empress, go to 33.

To try to escape from the palace, go to 17.

To touch all three horns together, go to 11.

26

"Golden Heart Crown, take me home!" you cry.

A kaleidoscope of coloured light and golden stars engulf you as you pass through time and space. You find yourself back in the Grotto of Light where Lady Harmony looks disappointed. "You must have made a wrong decision," she says. "Think carefully next time you have a choice to make."

Once again you make your way to the border and the magical wall of colour.

To try to break through it by force, go to 46.

To use magic to break through, go to 10.

27

"I surrender myself to you," you tell the black bears.

The leader speaks. "You have chosen wisely. Follow us. We will take you to the empress."

If you want to be taken to the empress, go to 19.

If you want to use your magic powers, go to 47.

28

"You will never destroy our rainbow," you tell the empress.

She laughs. "Oh, little unicorn, how wrong you are! My forces are already gathering on the border of our lands. Without your red unicorn, the rainbow will soon fade away and the wall of colour will vanish. With the barrier gone, I will conquer your kingdom and you can do nothing to stop me!"

Go to 42.

29

As the giant brings down the axe, you dodge aside and the sharp blade slices through the chain, freeing you!

To flee from the palace, go to 43.
To try to rescue Carmine, go to 25.

You remember that the goblins told you of a secret passageway through the waterfall.

Carefully you walk towards the rushing water, making sure that you are not swept off into the raging torrent below.

Following the pathway, you pass through the waterfall into a dark tunnel.

"Light!" you command. The tunnel lights up and you cry out in shock. A gigantic white spider crouches in your way! It shoots lines of thick, silken threads at you. Before you can respond, your legs and hooves are bound together and you topple over onto the stony ground.

To use your horn to try to cut through the threads, go to 13.

To try to use your magic powers, go to 38.

31

You gallop through the greyness of the Land of Shadows. Crows and ravens fly overhead and you wonder if they are spying on you.

After some time travelling, you arrive at the edge of a great forest. There is a pathway through the trees, but the way ahead is dark.

To head down the forest track, go to 12.
If you want to try to find a way around the forest, go to 44.

32

You call upon your magical powers and a stream of bright blue light shoots towards the knight. It hits your enemy, but nothing happens!

The black knight laughs. "My armour is made from shadownets; your unicorn magic will not work against me."

To attack the knight, go to 15.
To use your magic powers once more, go to 22.

33

You charge towards the empress, but a giant steps in your way, holding a shadownet in his great big hands.

He throws it towards you, but luckily you manage to avoid it. You race back to Emerald and Carmine as the giant picks up the net and heads towards you.

"What about using our horns?" Emerald suggests quickly.

Go to 11.

34

You rear up and flail your hooves at the goblins as they close in holding their short swords and spears. You knock several enemies down, but there are too many of them to fight at once. A couple of the goblins throw a shadownet over you. These powerful nets stop you using your unicorn magic.

You are trapped!

Go to 26.

35

You gallop along the track and leap over the tree trunk. As you land there is a crashing noise and you find yourself being hauled upwards in a shadownet.

It was a trap! You are hanging in the air, helpless to do anything. You glance below and see a troop of giggling goblins moving towards you armed with swords and spears.

Go to 26.

36

You gallop away as fast as you can, but the bears are too quick for you. They follow you and soon you are surrounded.

If you wish to use your magic to fight the bears, go to 47.

If you decide to surrender, go to 27.

37

You and Emerald head to the Grotto of Light, where Lady Harmony rules over the elves.

You explain the situation. Lady Harmony looks worried. "I will consult my magic crystal to see what has happened to Carmine."

She touches a large crystal on a stone pedestal. "Show me what has befallen the red unicorn," she demands.

The crystal reveals a series of images. You see some goblins breaking out of a tunnel they have dug under the magical wall dividing Rainbow Land from the Land of Shadows.

The crystal shows the goblins capturing Carmine and taking her back to their land!

If you have seen enough, go to 24.
If you wish to see more, go to 7.

38

Before you can use your magical powers, the spider leaps forward and plunges its fangs into your back. You feel the venom spreading through your body.

You can hardly move!

Go to 26.

39

You carry on for miles, but there is no end to the thousands of black trees. You are very tired now, so you stop for a moment. You see another track leading into the forest.

If you wish to rest, go to 3.

If you wish to head down the forest track, go to 12.

40

You break free of your captor's grip and race towards Carmine, hoping to slice through her chain with your horn.

"Stop that unicorn!" screams the empress

leaping up from her throne. A giant steps in your way, blocking your path to Carmine, and grabs hold of your neck.

If you want to try to use your magic unicorn powers, go to 8.

If you'd prefer to return to the Grotto of Light, go to 26.

41

You decide to follow the river away from the mountains. As you trot carefully through the dark meadowlands you see flocks of ravens and crows collecting directly above you. They circle overhead as they are joined by magpies and jackdaws. In the midst of all these swirling birds is a great white eagle.

There is a loud cry and you look up to see the eagle diving towards you. The other birds follow it. You are under attack!

To try and outrun the birds, go to 20.
To use your magic, go to 9.

42

The image of the empress disappears.

You turn to Lady Harmony. "We must rescue Carmine before the rainbow fades and our land turns to black and white. Emerald and I will travel to the Land of Shadows and rescue her."

Lady Harmony shakes her head. "No — if both of you go, the colours of the rainbow will fade more quickly. One of you must stay. Only one can go."

Both you and Emerald immediately volunteer to be the one.

Lady Harmony holds up her hand. "I will choose."

If you spoke to the empress, go to 18.
If you didn't, go to 49.

43

You race towards the marble doors, but before you can reach them, they are slammed shut.

"Kill the unicorn!" orders the empress.

Your enemies move in to obey her command.

Go to 26.

44

You decide that the way through the forest is too dangerous, so you gallop along the edge. The forest is vast and its blackness goes on seemingly forever. You travel for hours and hours and are getting tired.

If you wish to rest, go to 3.
If you wish to carry on, go to 39.

45

You charge at the knight, head lowered, but the rhinoceros simply knocks you down with a heavy blow.

The knight's evil laughter echoes in your ears.

You lie winded on the ground as the knight moves towards you on the rhinoceros's back.

To continue your attack, go to 15.
To use magic, go to 32.

46

You lower your head and charge at the wall. Your horn breaks the barrier and you pass through the large hole you created. But as you enter the Land of Shadows you realise that you have made a mistake!

A troop of goblins is waiting behind some bushes! They see the hole in the wall and race towards it.

To close the hole in the wall, go to 21.
To fight the goblins, go to 34.

47

You call on your magical powers, but nothing happens!

You glance into the pool of water and gasp in horror — your horn is slowly turning from blue to black — you realise that without Carmine and Emerald, the power of the rainbow that you control is fading and so are your magical powers.

You have to act quickly!

Go to 26.

48

Your horn turns brilliant blue and a stream of glittering stars bursts from it. The stars cover the goblins, trapping them in a net of sapphire-coloured light. They curse and threaten you, waving their fists, but they can do nothing.

If you want to question the goblins, go to 16.

If you wish to continue your search for Carmine, go to 31.

49

Lady Harmony looks at both you and Emerald. "The crystal shall decide," she says.

She waves her hand. "Magic crystal, show the way, who should go and who should stay?"

A beam of light swirls from the crystal and envelops you.

"The crystal has chosen," says Lady Harmony. Emerald looks disappointed.

"We need you here to protect the rainbow," you tell her. "Don't worry, I will bring Carmine back."

Go to 4.

50

You return to the Rainbow Land with Emerald and Carmine.

Lady Harmony meets you in the Grotto of Light. "Congratulations, unicorns! You have brought peace and colour to this realm. There is no longer a Land of Shadows and Yin Yang is banished forever. We will live in a land where all colours are loved. You are all heroes!"

Immortals

HERO

I HERO Quiz

Test yourself with this special
quiz. It has been designed to see
how much you remember about
the book you've just read. Can
you get all five answers right?

To download the answer sheets simply visit:

www.hachettechildrens.co.uk

Enter the "Teacher Zone" and search
"Immortals".

Question 1

What are the names of the three unicorns?

A   Sapphire, Carmine and Ruby

B   Carmine, Emerald and Garnet

C   Emerald, Topaz and Jade

D   Sapphire, Carmine and Emerald

Question 2

What does Lady Harmony first see in her magic crystal?

A   the goblins capturing Carmine

B   Empress Yin Yang

C   the goblins capturing Emerald

D   the Dark Palace

Question 3

Which animal is the black knight sitting astride?

A   an elephant

B   a bear

C   a rhinoceros

D   a white eagle

Question 4

What must the unicorns touch together
to renew the Rainbow Land rainbow?

A   their hooves

B   their horns

C   their tails

D   their noses

Question 5

Where do you find Lady Harmony?

A   Grotto of Light

B   Rainbow Grotto

C   Dark Palace

D   Gloomy Mountains

About the 2Steves

"The 2Steves" are Britain's most popular writing double act for young people, specialising in comedy and adventure. They perform regularly in schools and libraries, and at festivals, taking the power of words and story to audiences of all ages.

Together they have written many books, including the *Crime Team* series.
Find out what they've been up to at:
www.the2steves.net

About the illustrator: Jack Lawrence

Jack Lawrence is a successful freelance comics illustrator, working on titles such as *A.T.O.M.*, Cartoon Network, *Doctor Who Adventures*, *2000 AD*, *Transformers* and *Spider-Man Tower of Power*. He also works as a freelance toy designer.

Jack lives in Maidstone in Kent with his partner and two cats.

Have you completed the I HERO Quests?

Battle with aliens in Tyranno Quest:

AIR BLAST
Steve Barlow - Steve Skidmore
978 1 4451 0875 9 pb
978 1 4451 1345 6 ebook

FIRE STORM
Steve Barlow - Steve Skidmore
978 1 4451 0876 6 pb
978 1 4451 1346 3 ebook

ICE STRIKE
Steve Barlow - Steve Skidmore
978 1 4451 0877 3 pb
978 1 4451 1347 0 ebook

EARTH ATTACK
Steve Barlow - Steve Skidmore
978 1 4451 0878 0 pb
978 1 4451 1348 7 ebook

Defeat the Red Queen in Blood Crown Quest:

SANDS of BLOOD
Steve Barlow - Steve Skidmore
978 1 4451 1499 6 pb
978 1 4451 1503 0 ebook

DRAGON MOUNTAIN
Steve Barlow - Steve Skidmore
978 1 4451 1500 9 pb
978 1 4451 1504 7 ebook

DEMON SEA
Steve Barlow - Steve Skidmore
978 1 4451 1501 6 pb
978 1 4451 1505 4 ebook

CITY OF THE DEAD
Steve Barlow - Steve Skidmore
978 1 4451 1502 3 pb
978 1 4451 1506 1 ebook

Save planet Earth in Atlantis Quest:

MENACE FROM THE DEEP
Steve Barlow - Steve Skidmore
978 1 4451 2867 2 pb
978 1 4451 2868 9 ebook

OCEAN ALLIANCE
Steve Barlow - Steve Skidmore
978 1 4451 2870 2 pb
978 1 4451 2871 9 ebook

BATTLE FOR THE SEAS
Steve Barlow - Steve Skidmore
978 1 4451 2876 4 pb
978 1 4451 2877 1 ebook

ATLANTIS ASSAULT
Steve Barlow - Steve Skidmore
978 1 4451 2873 3 pb
978 1 4451 2874 0 ebook

More I HERO Immortals